# Englisch lernen mit Kurzgeschichten

Mit dieser Kurzgeschichte kannst du deine Englischkenntnisse schnell und einfach verbessern

Adam Winterspoon

1. Auflage

2019



ISBN: 9781081499402

# Inhaltsverzeichnis

# THE ADVENTURE

The land of opportunity. The land of freedom where everything is possible. I grew up idolizing the United States of America from their culture, their language to their democracy, name everything about it and it was all on my fingertips.

A twenty-year-old polish who had nothing but a theater of dreams influenced by all the American media content I had consumed in my younger years. Now it was all possible to live the American dream but wait, it could not just happen at the snap of a finger. This was a marathon and I had to practice first before running it otherwise, I would pull a muscle. First things first, language is the top cream of the American culture. The English language seduced me as a woman with all the possibilities it held, all the emotions and details it could express no other language could. No wonder Americans are so expressive, the versatility of their language enables it and so my mind was set on learning the English language and not just any English, the American English. So how does an unrefined Scandinavian youth like me psych themselves?

Being in a technological era, I quickly rushed to Google. On top of my search list was short stories audios books and pop music.

At least I had gotten one of them right since I was pop music fanatic and by a fanatic, I mean singing out Justin Bieber, Rihanna and Selena Gomez songs lyric after lyric. That was progress already. I was left with exploring audiobooks and short stories. Being a Scandinavian, English books in the country were scarce. Our nation insisted on the value of learning and owning a singular national language and so then Polish was my first and mother language by default.

Audiobooks seemed to be my only salvation, with my little IT knowledge, I knew I could download some from the foreign sites on Basic English and pronunciation. My first audiobook was "Basic English for first-time learners” I would listen to it literally, every time I had a chance. I was naturally a slow learner so I programmed myself to be listening to a paragraph each day and repeat it a few times then internalize it. The audio emphasized the importance of accent and hence I had to put on a New Yorker accent. Various greetings such as "Hi", "Good morning", "Good evening" is what I mostly got. After some time, I realized it was easy to forget some words even though I had practiced them long enough, but my failure to use them daily contributed to a low level of cognition. I started taking notes to enhance my active listening, which I could refer to when I forgot any single word.

Over time, my learning advanced to reading along with the audio from my notes to practice the accent and pronunciations. This meant stopping the recording once in a while and reproduce what I heard aloud to match the diction of what I just heard.

Grotezka, an aging old veteran who was popular in the village for having served in the U.N with three tours to his name, was a below-average English speaker. He was able to acquire the language from his comrades during the war. Hence, I gathered up courage and tried to indulge him on how best to learn the English language. From then on, we could communicate using our poorly pronounced English without any judgment. I went further ahead to discuss with him some chapters that proved to be challenging in the audiobook.

During snowy winter afternoons, we could light a fire in his cabin and discuss wide topics strictly using English. He corrected me and I did the same too. I was the greatest winner as I was practicing how to use the newly learned words in sentences and slowly developed the courage to speak my heavily accented English.

The audiobooks had opened up so many possibilities and my basic language skills were progressing at a tremendous rate. I could comfortably greet, applaud and exclaim in English.

The language itself was drowning, it obsessed me and audiobooks were becoming too ordinary for me. Time had come to take up a new challenge if I was to improve my language skills. The burning desire to become a linguist coupled with my mathematics and science enthusiasm led me to apply for a scholarship in the U.S.A to further my studies. I had completed my four-year vocational High School and was considering prospective career paths given my average grades.

The research for a scholarship commenced. It was a vigorous exercise that consumed most of my time searching for possible sponsoring institutions in the USA. My long search led me to one institution, in particular, known as the Anthony and Josephine Chumura College. It specifically desired a candidate of polish descent. This was it, my one ticket to freedom as I was a perfect fit for the profile. I submitted my application with all the necessary attachments and payments. After two months, they offered me a chance in the institution under an Anthony and Josephine Science scholarship program.

I was to pursue Bachelors in Mathematical sciences under a full scholarship covering my boarding, tuition and upkeep expenses. Everything had worked out perfectly and it felt like all my childhood prayers came through. I could barely contain myself, waiting for the day to move to a new life order.

American visas were hard enough to obtain but for my case, since it was a study endeavor, the interview was short and successful and I was granted a five-year study visa. My flight ticket was sent and all I was left to do was wait, which turned out to be the hardest part. Curiosity and excitement were burning inside me. On the material day of my flight, I knew it was the last day my feet were graced by my motherland Poland. The smell of the air, the chilly breezes was the last caresses I savored. At the Warsaw

Chopin Airport My folks, especially my dad did not cease to remind me that I will always be Pole, blood and bone. He insisted on never to forget my roots for a tree with weak roots will always be short-lived.

My ears were clogged most of the time due to my loud heartbeats coming to terms with the fact that I was opening a brand new chapter in my life. Everything I knew, everything I thought was reality was soon about to change.

The American dream was edging closer and I could see it embracing me. As the plane took off, it left a part of me at that airport. My mother in her brown scarf wrapped around her head, face buried in her hands soaked in tears was hoping to see me come back as a scientist, but her dreams were not my dreams.

The flight took seventy-two hours but with connecting flights at Amsterdam and Berlin cities that I only learned in my geography class. Finally, it landed at Los

Angeles Airport and the thuds inside my chest got harder and harder, this was a new me as I stepped out of the plane descending the stairs. My heartbeat had already increased. It symbolized a rebirth into a new world; even for me, it was overwhelming.

The Anthony and Josephine Chumura Organization had already sent one of their senior students to receive me at the Airport. It was not hard finding him because he had worn a big board written, "Anthony and Josephine Chumura Organization welcome to America". Anthony and Josephine Chumura was the couple behind the sponsorship program. The couple had moved to the states at a young age and enjoyed a successful science scholarly career going through top state universities in America and eventually hanging the boots to pursue philanthropic activities supporting young ambitious polish scientists.

It was an honor to be included in their vision and be a beneficiary of the same. The fact that a senior polish student was receiving me made it even more breathtaking. His name was Syzmon, 3rd year in the School of Informatics.

When he spoke to welcome me, I was surprised that his polish accent was light, a few more years and he could speak almost as good as a Native American.

We boarded his car and drove to the institution, which was situated in Brooklyn, New York.

All along the ride, I was silent as I was lost in the awe and amazement that I was processing.

The skyscrapers in the well laid out clean streets, teenagers driving at the age of sixteen. It was small heaven in my eyes. Before I realized it, we had already arrived though it was late. We had supper and due to the jet lag, I went straight to bed in an already prepared room. I promised myself though that I would tour the city from corner to corner the next day. The following day was much of paperwork, where I filled so many forms until it was annoying. Later on, I headed to the international students' office, where I met with my supervisor and had a thorough counseling session revolving around orientation to my new institution and the conduct, that is expected of me as an international student. There was also the minimum grade attainment I should achieve to proceed to the next semester. Above all, everyone was nice and friendly with each of them willing to offer a helping hand. The day was full of activities so much that it was already nightfall. Los Angeles is an amazing city, specifically at night with glittering lights all around. From my room's window, I could view the many-colored lights appearing like a galaxy.

The noise of the nightlife with modern pop and techno clubs was beckoning me to join them, but I had to restrain myself as a spectator tonight. All along, communication was mostly in polish, it was amazing how they reserved our Pole values even in the middle of an entirely different world. The rest of the college was speaking in English.

This would be an opportune moment to practice my little English because the environment and socialism pressured it. People in the US were friendly and open, with smiley faces all over wishing you a good day. In my efforts to respond to their wishes, they could notice my heavy accent and smile even harder. I could not figure out completely whether it was my face or accent that amused them all the same what mattered is that they were ready to embrace me in their society.

The next few mornings before I registered for my course units, I would undertake during my semester. I would take early walks to diners to take my breakfast. Along with the pavements walking, I practiced most of my greetings as I said "Hi" to every passerby I met.

My introduction consisted of "Hi, my name is Aleksander, how are you doing today?" with responses followed by "Fine, thank you". The same warmth I gave to every stranger I received it back in ten folds. I was able to perfect my greeting at any time of the day. Unlike in Poland, the US had a special place for greetings, it was culture to take time and know-how your fellow citizen is doing. The diner I frequented was five hundred yards from my school hostels and I enjoyed the morning walks followed by listening over to conversations in the diner.

I became a regular so much that I even had a reserved sitting spot at the counter where a young mid-twenties brunette female named Sandy always served me or at least that is what the nametag of her uniform read. My regular order was a cup of hot steamy gourmet coffee and pancakes with syrup.

I could not help but notice how her checked red and black uniform fit her perfectly with long hair spreading over her shoulders and the smile she would always put on while serving. There was barely any exchange of words between only short glances, friendly beams and us. However, I looked hard and long as she walked to the backroom to pick up the order and later pretend to be watching the news on her way back with the order.

The diner was full of Native Americans and I was shy of speaking such broken English among refined fluent compatriots. What was weird about it all was that most conversations I overhead actually helped me discover some new words. Words that were commonly used to refer to things.

With my notebook, I noted each one of them and the context under which usually they applied.

I would later on go and ask Syzmon who explained each one of them to me and helped me to practice them in conversations. He would usually make fun of my gusto before he agreed to assist. Finally, I registered my course units after a week and I was set for classes. To my surprise, all classes were in English but being a science aficionado, I took it as a challenge. Though it was difficult as most mathematics and science books were written in English. Very few of them translated to English. This pushed my need to learn the language and so I had to sign up for the English focus course.

Its duration was running for four weeks with twelve hours of study per week. The program was a multi-skill focusing attention on English grammar development together with academic writing and reading.

This course helped me understand the structure of the English language and not just speaking random words. I was now able to use them when deemed appropriate.

We learned about alphabets, vowels, parts of speech, punctuation, and tenses. Learning English as a subject illuminated some light on its academic aspect beyond its spoken ability. It became much clearer, that spoken and written English are two different aspects of the language.

Written English was more detailed and delicate where only certain words would be combined with others for the statement to make perfect sense. English had a set of rules to adhere to for it to become fluent and correct these set of rules are what we were exploring in detail.

Unlike spoken English, written English was tough and required literal studying, content-based studying and group assignments. For spoken English, we would do grammar and vocabulary presentations every week where we practiced on pronunciations. It went to an extent of simulating real-world social interactions and role-playing in class to ease ourselves into the language transitions. At first, it seemed difficult but other students did not have any background of the language unlike me.

This motivated me to put in all my effort. It became more interesting as different international students with their accents joined the class. We would often find humor in different accents, especially Chinese and Russian accents. It led me to have some pride in my own. An accent was a unique identifier of the effect of your mother language on your second language and it was nothing to make you ashamed. Towards the end of the semester, I could now comfortably fit in an English math lecture and intake almost one hundred percent of what the lecturers delivered.

With my new improved English, I had now full confidence to start random conversations with strangers at my favorite diner spot. Middle-aged folks dominated the diner. They mostly discussed American politics and critic every decision Donald Trump was making. I pretended to understand what was going on in the political scene but it was in an attempt to continue growing and nurturing my social interactions in the English language. When the political debates got too boring and personal, I decided to chitchat Sandy, my favorite waiter.

She had now noticed I was changed and not my usual silent self. Due to her busy schedule, we could only make casual jokes as she served me. She could not even sit down to share a cup of coffee.

The diner was a favorite spot for most folks, so she was working around the clock. I had to be more creative in my means of creating quality time with her.

One morning, I woke up very early at five thirty and decided to spare some few minutes to talk to her since a conversation while she was serving the customers during the day was impossible. I dressed up warmly in the cold windy dusk Friday morning and stood beside the diner's entrance. I saw her approaching at a distance of thirty yards and she quickly noticed me back. "Ooooooooh Aleksander what are you doing here at this time of the morning?", she asked. I smiled faintly and answered in a Polish accent "I am here to see you."

She acted surprised but deep down in her guts, she felt the warmth that glowed through her eyes. She brought out a bunch of keys from her handbag and opened the diner's door though still making some significant eye contact with me. That moment, right there was priceless, in the silence of the morning with our gesture giving out mixed signals to each other felt special. I could not explain it but a warm feeling was attached to it. It was better than turning in bed waiting for the sun rays to pierce through my window. I would have given anything for more mornings such as this. We walked into the diner and without even a moment of hesitation, she asked what I wanted to talk about.

Our conversation started with introductions and detailed explanations of our backgrounds.

After sharing on my craving interest to learn the English language, she offered me a new secret of learning English even deeper but made me wait until the next day. It was one of the longest waits though I do not know why ladies always have to make a gent wait for something. Is it a test of patience, or a test of determination I could not quite figure it out but whatever the cost, I had no choice but to wait. The next morning I went down to the diner anxious about the so-called secret, which I later found out, was a book.

To make matters more interesting the book was a children's short story book. It hit me by surprise that she would recommend a book, which was beneath me, and honestly speaking it was a disappointing surprise but in her justifications, she explained that if I was to speak English perfectly the power was in reading. According to her, the children's book was the best way to start. All the same, I felt belittled deep inside but still saw it as a sweet gesture from her and so I read the storybook and completed it. When I tried to give it back she insisted that I read it a second and third time which I still did although half-heartedly. The storybook helped me connect my sentences well.

Most statements I was making were disconnected and, usually lost sense along the way. This was a major milestone and it seemed like English was an ocean that had unimaginable depths. That part of me hungry and starving to master English could not be satisfied and, so the venture went on deeper and deeper. The more I learned, the more I craved eventually Sandy and I became close because now I made it a habit of asking her to recommend my next book. The good thing is that she was a reader too and it inspired me to soar up to her heights.

The love for books was creating a bond between us that we never saw coming. On weekends, we had a special spot in the park where we would both read our respective books and share a little on what we have read. The discussions were deep, insightful and intellectual. However, in the midst of it all, we could steal some light kisses and warm breaths on each other skins all in the name of English.

Some intimacy was built behind the books, which led to our first date. It had been weeks since she started me on the children short story books and now I was leveled up to science fiction books, as of course science was my first love. On our first date, I saw Sandy differently as a woman who had accepted me in my original nature and was trying to convert me to a decently-refined linguist.

As much as it was little progress, it had a big impact on me. The first date led to the second date and the second date to the third date. Fun, low-key romance, free expression, cheap thrills were what graced our dates. The company superseded our date locations it was about me being close to her and her being close to me. Officially, we were a couple, officially, we were dating, officially, she was mine and I was hers. What started as a book challenge, turned into a steamy love affair. To me, this was an inconceivable reality that English had sunk me in and it was beautiful, simply beautiful.

Now words were no longer just words, they had a deeper and figurative meaning. My choice words determined how well I expressed myself and, Sandy helped me have that breakthrough in our intimacy.

I used the same language to express how alive she made me feel. How she seemed like a fairy tale and I was the knight in shining armor coming to rescue her. She did the same too and those words moved us together. I was in a relationship with her but all along it felt like we were the three of us, Sandy, English and I. English was our connecting node, our midpoint, where all our feelings could directly flow. It was our bridge, our baseline. At school, the same language excellence reflected in my academics.

I was soon leading the class. Mathematical sciences had an aspect of language in them and it could not be achieved without true mastery of the language. Researching on mathematics books written in English majorly contributed to this masterly.

When asked to explain or present mathematical theories, the same language empowered me to explain them in the simplest and accurate form.

One and a half years down the line and English had opened up so many opportunities in my new life.

One most important piece in this process of growth was Sandy who also had a hidden passion for language and I brought it out as we shared and challenged each other. She suggested that we scale up our language standards to the point of intellectualism and artistic abilities. We decided to be attending plays, theatre performances, and poem narrations. A few blocks down the streets from the diner, there was a community theatre, which was open to anyone who felt the need to explore performing arts. Most locals dismissed the theatre as an avenue for amateurs but we respected any ideology an individual had on language, hence it was important to accord them a fair chance to prove themselves. We were there mainly to listen but not to perform. I found artistic language written on scripts very deep and emotional. It had a way of bringing out all the unspoken emotions.

I could not help but examine it deeper. We also became good fans of TV shows, TV series, and any lyrically deep music. Our interest was on the respective scripts and the language used to write the emotions they intended to induce. Saturday nights officially became theatre nights for Sandy and I.

It became a way to go out and at the same time enrich our language. The theatre was barely filled by any audience as it was old and the community itself was not fervent about the same. We became regulars at the theatre to a point the directors knew our names and could wait for us to commence any performance. Further interaction enabled us to learn how scriptwriters feel every word they write. Every word is a part of a whole system with its role. We were so engaged that it even affected our speech between us and among other people. Sunday night became our movie night too where we would pick the best top rated script movies, paying a keen interest on the character's speech. Language had expanded my thinking dimension; it had also enhanced my relations with others.

I found it easier to make friends by creating fun conversations with them, which made me likable. Words seemed to unlock people's hearts and warm up to them. In turn, I started enjoying being social and broke out of my introvert cocoon.

This time I had the right words for every situation and my presence could be felt among people by my speech. This led to my election as a student's leader by the other students as a representative of international students. It felt fulfilling that I could serve my comrades at an official capacity. Public speaking was my newfound hobby that extended my leadership into other forums.

If this was the kind of magic that English worked in my life then I would not need anything else.

My obsession with English, however, created a disconnect with my Polish culture. English was American and American was English. The less frequent I spoke Pole, the less my cultural background meant. I had always admired America but at no point did I want to lose my polish persona. My Polish college mates warned me about this and it hit me hard when I realized, I had never spoken

Pole for a while. This was a challenge to me and was forcing me to stick and stand by one language. However, I came to the compromise of having them in equal measure. To enhance this ability to be fluent and able to change tongues in an instant, I took up translation classes where I learned to translate Polish to English and vice versa.

The distinctiveness of the two languages was clear. My main aim for doing this was to find a connection between the two languages and not lose Polish in an attempt to master English. To be a balanced individual who could speak both languages fluently. It represented a part of who I was and who I wanted to become.

In my final year of study, I had gotten used to the US, so much that leaving was too difficult. My visa was going to expire soon and, I would be forced to go back to Poland. Not that I held anything against being in Poland but I felt there was more for me to adventure in the USA. After serious considerations, I decided to start a podcast. Podcasts were a new trend of mass media popularly known as "radio on-demand". The whole idea was to reach out to any Polish coming into America and guiding them into having a fruitful life here. I had to sort my visa issue first and applied for a work permit to enable me to find work and live on my own.

Most students under scholarship had it rough when desiring to extend their stay in the states. When scholarship durations expired, you were expected to go back to your country and apply for a different visa as a citizen who wants to work in the USA.

The hustles of all the procedure of extending my visa and work permit led to one crazy idea.

Mother of all crazy ideas and again it was coming from Sandy who I shared with my visa ordeal. She made a casual suggestion that we get married so that I would become a citizen by naturalization forcing me to stay in the USA as long as I desired.

It was scary because marriage should be out of love and not convenience but didn't

I love Sandy? Didn't we spend enough time together? Didn't we bond enough at deeper levels? I had to trust her gut on this and make a decision first since my visa was almost expired. Yes, I purposed it in my heart that I would marry her. Also, our marriage would not be one of those fancy ones but just a simple civil union at the Attorney's General office.

We headed down to the civil offices in the company of my two witnesses who were Syzmon and Podolski. While she brought along her two sisters to attest to our union, this is not how I probably had imagined it, the entire process of meeting and marrying a woman was supposed to be special and perfect, I kept reminding myself that it's all for my good and in the name of love.

The ceremony was short, we made our vows and signed the marriage certificates. Automatically I officially became an American citizen. Most of all I was to be with Sandy for the rest of my life. I moved in with her, in her one-bedroom studio In Brooklyn.

Now I could pursue my podcast plans, I was determined to touch the hearts of young Polish youths and ease their transition to the USA.

My first challenge was to find a suitable name for my podcast and decided it will go by "The Polish Podcast, for poles by poles" my content was largely based on the air of barroom banter custom-produced for foreigners looking to move to the USA for work or study. I decided to spice it up with interviews of various Poles who moved to the US and how life here is suiting them so far. I also shared some Poland culture and pride like the Polish-jazz and some polish delicacies.

I was marketing Poland in the USA and at the same time praising the hospitality of the states to foreigners. It was not easy to build a fan base but my listeners were mostly poles from my college and Sandy had also convinced the diner management to let the customers listen in instead of the usual political banter.

The podcast is where I shared all my amazing experiences of my stay in

America, encouraging anyone with dreams of coming here to wake up and chase them. It was amazing the heights I had scaled all courtesy of my ambitions of the English language.

Sandy and I were working out fine and due to my excellent grades, I was offered a contractual tutor assignment at the college to assist any students who had difficulties in class.

My graduation was a colorful ceremony with mama and papa flying in from Poland to share in my success. Looking back to the far I have come, I owe it to a little fire in me that sparkled when I discovered the English language.

# DAS ABENTEUER

Das Land der Möglichkeiten. Das Land der Freiheit, in dem alles möglich ist. Ich bin damit aufgewachsen, die Vereinigten Staaten von Amerika von ihrer Kultur, ihrer Sprache bis zu ihrer Demokratie zu verehren.

Ein zwanzigjähriger Pole der nichts als einen Traum hatte, beeinflusst von all den amerikanischen Medien, welche ich in meinen jungen Jahren konsumiert hatte. Jetzt war es möglich, den amerikanischen Traum zu leben, aber warten Sie, es konnte nicht einfach mit einem Fingerschnipsen geschehen. Es war ein Marathon und ich musste erst trainieren bevor ich ihn laufen konnte. Ansonsten würde ich mir einen Muskelriss zuziehen.

Das Wichtigste zuerst: Die Sprache ist die Creme de la Creme der amerikanischen Kultur. Die englische Sprache verführte mich mit all ihren Emotionen wie es sonst keine Sprache konnte. Kein Wunder, dass die Amerikaner so ausdrucksstark sind, die Vielseitigkeit ihrer Sprache ermöglicht dies.

So war ich bestrebt, das amerikanische Englisch zu lernen.

Wie stellt das jedoch ein skandinavischer Jugendlicher wie ich selbst an?

Da ich mich in einer technologischen Ära befand, eilte ich schnell zu Google. Ganz oben in der Suchliste standen Kurzgeschichten, Hörbücher und Popmusik.

Ich war ein Popmusikfanatiker, der Songtexte von Justin Bieber, Rihanna und Selena Gomez auswendig beherrschte. Für mich war das bereits ein Fortschritt. Ich blieb mit der Erforschung von Hörbüchern und Kurzgeschichten zurück.

Als Skandinavier waren englische Bücher im Land knapp. In unserer Nation lernte man normalerweise nur eine einzige Sprache, somit war Polnisch die einzige Sprache die ich beherrschte.

Hörbücher schienen meine einzige Rettung zu sein. Mit meinen kleinen PC-Kenntnissen wusste ich, dass ich einige von den ausländischen Büchern über die Grundlagen der englischen Sprache und Aussprache herunterladen konnte.

Mein erstes Hörbuch war „Basic English for first-time learners";, ich hörte es buchstäblich immer, wenn ich etwas Freizeit hatte. Ich war leider ein langsam Lernender, also nahm ich mir vor, jeden Tag einen Absatz zu hören.

Verschiedene Grüße wie „Hi";, „Guten Morgen";, „Guten Abend"; habe ich mir am leichtesten merken können. Nach einigen Tagen merkte ich, dass ich zuvor gelernte Wörter und Ausdrücke schnell vergessen habe. Ich fing also an, Notizen zu machen, um so effektiver lernen zu können. Im Laufe der Zeit entwickelte sich meine Aussprache und mein Akzent wurde immer schwächer. Immer wieder stoppte ich das Hörbuch, um den gerade gehörten Satz laut auszusprechen.

Grotezka, ein alter Veteran, welcher in meinem Dorf sehr beliebt war, beherrschte als einziger ein wenig die englische Sprache. Er konnte die Sprache während des Krieges von seinen Kameraden erlernen. Daher sammelte ich Mut, ging zu ihm und fragte ihn wie man die englische Sprache am besten lernen könne.

Von diesem Tag an konnten wir mit unserem schlecht ausgeprägten Englisch kommunizieren. Ich bat ihn zum Beispiel bei komplizierten Kapiteln des Buches um Hilfe.

An schneereichen Winternachmittagen konnten wir in seiner Wohnung ein Feuer anzünden und gemütlich über die verschiedensten Themen auf Englisch reden. Bei sprachlichen Fehlern hat er mich korrigiert und ich habe das Selbe bei ihm getan. Ich war ein echter Champion, was das einbauen von neuen Wörtern in Sätze anging. Die Hörbücher hatten mir viele Möglichkeiten eröffnet, und meine grundlegenden Sprachkenntnisse schritten enorm schnell voran. Ich konnte bequem begrüßen, applaudieren und auf Englisch ausrufen. Ich interessierte mich immer mehr für die englische Sprache und Hörbücher wurden für mich zur Gewohnheit. Es war an der Zeit, eine neue Herausforderung anzunehmen, wenn ich meine Sprachkenntnisse verbessern wollte.

Der brennende Wunsch, Linguist zu werden, gepaart mit meiner mathematischen und naturwissenschaftlichen Begeisterung, veranlasste mich, mich für ein Stipendium in den USA zu bewerben, um mein Studium fortzusetzen.

Ich hatte mein vierjähriges berufliches Gymnasium abgeschlossen und überlegte, ob ich bei meinen Durchschnittsnoten einen zukünftigen Karriereweg einschlagen könnte. Die Suche nach einem Stipendium begann. Es war eine große Herausforderung, mögliche Sponsoringinstitutionen in den USA zu finden. Meine lange Suche führte mich zu einer Institution, dem Anthony and Josephine Chumura College. Sie wünschten sich ausdrücklich einen Kandidaten mit polnischer Abstammung. Das war es, mein einziges Ticket in die Freiheit. Ich habe meinen Antrag mit allen notwendigen Anlagen und Zahlungen eingereicht. Nach zwei Monaten boten sie mir eine Chance in der Institution im Rahmen eines Anthony and Josephine Science Stipendienprogramms.

Ich sollte einen Bachelor-Abschluss in Mathematikwissenschaften im Rahmen eines Vollstipendiums erwerben, welches meine Kosten für Unterkunft, Unterricht und Unterhalt abdeckte. Alles hatte perfekt funktioniert und es fühlte sich an, als wurden all meine Gebete erhört. Ich konnte es kaum erwarten und wartete gespannt auf den Tag der Tage.

Ein amerikanisches Visa war im Normalfall schwer zu bekommen, aber da es sich um ein Studienprojekt handelte, war das Interview kurz und erfolgreich. Somit erhielt ich glücklicherweise ein fünfjähriges Studienvisum. Mein Flugticket wurde mir zugeschickt. Ab jetzt hieß es warten, was sich als der schwierigste Teil der ganzen Geschichte herausstellte. Neugierde und Aufregung brannten in mir. Der Geruch der Luft, die kühle Brise waren die letzten Liebkosungen, die ich genoss.

Am Warschauer Flughafen Chopin haben mich meine Eltern, vor allem mein Vater, immer wieder daran erinnert, dass ich immer Pole sein werde. Er bestand darauf, meine Wurzeln nie zu vergessen, denn ein Baum mit schwachen Wurzeln wird nicht lange überleben. Der amerikanische Traum rückte näher und ich konnte sehen, wie er mich umarmte. Als das Flugzeug startete, ließ es einen Teil von mir an diesem Flughafen zurück. Meine Mutter in ihrem braunen Schal, der um den Kopf gewickelt war, das Gesicht in ihren Händen vergraben und von Tränen getränkt. Der Flug dauerte 72 Stunden, dies war den Anschlussflügen in den Städten Amsterdam und Berlin geschuldet.

Schließlich landete es am Los Angeles Airport, die Stöße in meiner Brust wurden immer härter. Es symbolisierte eine

Wiedergeburt in eine neue Welt; gerade für mich war es überwältigend. Die Anthony and Josephine Chumura Organisation hatte bereits einen ihrer älteren Schüler geschickt, um mich am Flughafen zu empfangen.

Es war nicht schwer, ihn zu finden, denn er hatte ein großes Brett getragen, auf welchem: „Anthony and Josephine Chumura Organization welcome to America"; stand. Anthony und Josephine Chumura waren das Paar hinter dem Sponsoringprogramm. Das Paar war in jungen Jahren in die Staaten gezogen und genoss eine erfolgreiche wissenschaftliche Karriere, indem es an staatlichen Spitzenuniversitäten in Amerika studierte um philanthropische Aktivitäten zur Unterstützung junger ehrgeiziger polnischer Wissenschaftler zu unternehmen. Es war mir eine Ehre, in ihre Vision einbezogen zu werden und davon zu profitieren.

Die Tatsache, dass ich von einem älteren polnischen Studenten empfangen wurde, machte es noch atemberaubender.

Sein Name war Syzmon, 3. Jahrgang an der Fakultät für Informatik.

Als er mich auf Englisch willkommen hieß, war ich über seinen leichten polnischen Akzent sehr überrascht. Wir stiegen in sein Auto und fuhren zu der Einrichtung, die sich in Brooklyn, New York, befand. Die ganze Fahrt über war ich still, da ich in der Ehrfurcht und dem Staunen, das sich in mir ausbreitete, gefangen war. Die Wolkenkratzer in den gut ausgebauten, sauberen Straßen, Teenager, die im Alter von sechzehn Jahren Auto fahren. Es war ein kleiner Himmel in meinen Augen.

Nach dem Abendessen ging ich wegen des Jetlags direkt ins Bett. Ich nahm mir jedoch vor, die Stadt am nächsten Tag genauestens zu erkunden.

Zuerst musste ich jedoch noch viele Formulare ausfüllen. Später ging ich ins Büro für internationale Studierende, wo ich mich mit meinem Betreuer traf und eine ausführliche Beratung durchführte, die sich mit der Orientierung an meiner neuen Hochschule und dem Verhalten, das von mir als internationaler Student erwartet wird, beschäftigte. Auch wurde das Mindestniveau angesprochen, welches ich erreichen musste, um zum nächsten Semester überzugehen. Alle Leute mit denen ich zu tun hatte waren sehr nett und freundlich.

Los Angeles ist eine erstaunliche Stadt, besonders nachts, mit funkelnden Lichtern rundum. Vom Fenster meines Zimmers aus konnte ich die vielfarbigen Lichter wie eine Galaxie bestaunen. Der Lärm des Nachtlebens mit modernen Pop- und Techno-Clubs weckte mich nachts gelegentlich, aber ich musste mich heute Abend als Zuschauer zurückhalten. Die meiste Zeit war die Kommunikation auf Polnisch, es war erstaunlich, wie sie unsere polnischen Werte auch inmitten einer völlig anderen Welt repräsentiert hatten. Der Rest des Colleges sprach auf Englisch. Dies wäre ein günstiger Moment gewesen, um mein schlechtes Englisch aufzubessern.

Die Menschen in den USA waren freundlich und offen. Lächelnde Gesichter, die dir einen guten Tag wünschten. Wenn sie dann meinen harten Akzent hörten, mussten die meisten noch mehr lächeln.

Manchmal war ich mir nicht ganz sicher ob es mein Akzent oder mein Gesicht war, der sie so amüsierte. Die Hauptsache war jedoch, dass sie bereit waren, mich in ihrer Gesellschaft aufzunehmen.

Ich machte frühe Spaziergänge zu den Restaurants, um mein Frühstück einzunehmen. Geimeinsam mit den neuen Wegen übte ich die neuen Grüße, indem ich jedem Passanten, den ich traf, „Hello"; sagte. Mein erster Satz lautete immer „Hello, my name is Aleksander, how are you today?".

Die gleiche Wärme, die ich jedem Fremden gab, erhielt ich in zehnfacher Ausführung zurück. Ich konnte meinen Gruß für jede Tageszeit perfektionieren. Im Gegensatz zu Polen gibt es in den USA einen besonderen Stellenwert für Begrüßungen. Das Abendessen war fünfhundert Meter von meiner Schulherberge entfernt, und ich genoss die Morgenspaziergänge, gefolgt von Gesprächen im Saal. Ich wurde so sehr Stammgast, dass ich sogar einen reservierten Sitzplatz an der Theke hatte, wo mich immer eine junge Frau namens Sandy bediente. Meine Standardbestellung war eine Tasse heißer, dampfender Gourmetkaffee und Pfannkuchen mit Sirup.

Im Saal sprachen alle perfekt Englisch und ich schämte mich, ein so gebrochenes Englisch unter gebildeten Landsleuten zu sprechen. Mit meinem Notebook notierte ich mir einige Wörter und Sätze, welche ich bei meinem Essen hörte.

Später würde ich Syzmon fragen, der mir jeden einzelnen von ihnen erklärte und mir half, sie in Gespräche einzubauen. Normalerweise machte er sich über meine Sprachkenntnisse lustig, bevor er mir half. Was den Unterricht anbelangt, war ich zuerst überrascht, denn wirklich alle Kurse waren auf Englisch. Aber als

Naturwissenschaftler nahm ich es als Herausforderung an.

Besonders schwierig war, dass die meisten mathematischen und naturwissenschaftlichen Bücher auf Englisch geschrieben waren. Dadurch wurde mein Drang Englisch zu lernen noch größer und ich meldete mich für den Englisch-Fokuskurs an. Die Kursdauer betrug vier Wochen mit zwölf Stunden Studium pro Woche.

Der Kurs war ein Multi-Skill-Programm, welches sich auf die Entwicklung der englischen Grammatik sowie auf akademisches Schreiben und Lesen konzentrierte. Dieser Kurs half mir, die Struktur der englischen Sprache zu verstehen und nicht nur zufällige Wörter zu sprechen. Wir lernten Vokale, Wortteile, Interpunktionen und Zeitformen kennen. In diesem Kurs wurde mir klar, dass gesprochenes und geschriebenes Englisch zwei verschiedene Welten sind. Das geschriebene Englisch war detaillierter und heikler, wobei nur bestimmte Wörter mit anderen kombiniert wurden, damit die Aussage einen vollkommenen Sinn macht.

Im Gegensatz zu gesprochenem Englisch war geschriebenes Englisch sehr schwierig und erforderte wörtliches Lernen, inhaltsbasiertes Lernen und Gruppenarbeiten. Für das gesprochene Englisch würden wir jede Woche Grammatik- und Vokabularvorträge halten, in denen wir die Aussprache üben. Es ging bis zu einem gewissen Grad darum, reale Interaktionen zu simulieren und Rollenspiele im Unterricht zu spielen, um sich in die Sprachübergänge einzuarbeiten.

Zuerst schien es schwierig, aber andere Schüler hatten im Gegensatz zu mir keinen Hintergrund der Sprache. Das motivierte mich, mit aller Kraft zu arbeiten. Es wurde immer interessanter, als verschiedene internationale Schüler mit ihren Akzenten in den Unterricht eintraten. Es war oft lustig, wenn verschiedene Akzente aufeinandertrafen, vor allem der chinesische und russische Akzent.

So entwickelte ich mit der Zeit ein wenig Stolz in Bezug auf meinen Akzent. Ein Akzent ist ein eindeutiger Identifikator für die Wirkung deiner Muttersprache in Bezug auf deine zweite Sprache, und es war nichts, wofür man sich schämen sollte. Gegen Ende des Semesters konnte ich mich nun bequem in eine englische Mathematikvorlesung setzen und fast hundert Prozent von dem, was die Dozenten vermittelten, aufnehmen.

Mit meinem neuen verbesserten Englisch hatte ich nun das volle Selbstvertrauen, zufällige Gespräche mit Fremden in meinem Lieblingsrestaurant zu beginnen. Die Leute mittleren Alters dominierten den Saal. Sie diskutierten hauptsächlich über die amerikanische Politik und kritisierten jede Entscheidung, die Donald Trump traf. Ich tat so, als würde ich verstehen, was in der politischen Szene vor sich ging und konnte mich so in das Gespräch einklinken.

Mit der Zeit wurden mir diese politischen Debatten jedoch zu langweilig. Also beschloss ich mit meiner Lieblingskellnerin Sandy zu plaudern. Sie hatte bereits bemerkt, dass ich mich verändert hatte. Mein Englisch war um Welten besser und ich war nicht mehr so schüchtern. Aufgrund ihres vollen Terminkalenders konnten wir jedoch nur Gelegenheitswitze machen, während sie mich bediente. Sie konnte sich nicht einmal hinsetzen, um eine Tasse Kaffee zu trinken. Das Restaurant war der Lieblingsplatz vieler Leute, also arbeitete sie rund um die Uhr.

Ich musste kreativer sein, um mit ihr einen guten Draht aufzubauen. Eines Morgens wachte ich sehr früh auf und entschied mich, ein paar Minuten mit ihr zu sprechen. Ein Gespräch, während sie tagsüber die Kunden bediente, war nämlich unmöglich. Ich zog mich an diesem kalten, windigen Freitagmorgen also warm an und ging zu dem Restaurant.

„Ooooooooooooh Aleksander, was machst du denn um diese Uhrzeit hier?";, fragte sie als ich durch die Tür ging. Ich lächelte schwach und antwortete mit polnischem Akzent: „Ich bin hier, um dich zu sehen. Sie reagierte zuerst etwas überrascht, aber in ihren Augen konnte ich sie innerlich lächeln sehen.

Für mich war es ein unbezahlbarer Moment. Wir warfen uns in der Stille des Morgens freudige Blicke zu. Ich konnte es nicht erklären, aber ich war innerlich erwärmt. Für solche Morgenstunden hätte ich schon früher alles gegeben.

Wir gingen ein Stück durch den Saal und ohne auch nur einen Moment zu zögern fragte sie, worüber ich denn reden wollte. Ich hatte keine wirkliche Antwort auf diese Frage und redete einfach los. Zuerst erzählte ich woher ich kam und warum ich hier sei. Ich erzählte ihr, dass ich die englische Sprache lernen und perfektionieren wollte. Sie meinte, dass sie zu diesem Thema ein Geheimnis habe. Ich musste jedoch bis zum nächsten Tag warten um dieses Geheimnis zu erfahren. War es ein Geduldstest oder ein Test der Entschlossenheit, ich konnte es nicht ganz verstehen, aber ich hatte keine andere Wahl, als zu warten.

Am nächsten Morgen ging ich in das Restaurant, um endlich das Geheimnis zu enthüllen. Dieses war zu meiner Enttäuschung lediglich ein Buch.

Der Fakt, dass es ein Kinder-Kurzgeschichtenbuch war, machte die Situation nicht gerade besser. Es überraschte mich, dass sie ein Buch empfiehl, welches scheinbar unter meinen Fähigkeiten lag. Sie erklärte jedoch, dass für perfektes Englisch  die Kraft im Lesen lag.

Laut ihr war das Kinderbuch der beste Einstieg. Trotzdem fühlte ich mich tief im Inneren herabgesetzt, sah es aber dennoch als eine süße Geste von ihr und so las ich das Bilderbuch. Als ich es ihr zurückgeben wollte, bestand sie darauf, dass ich es ein zweites und drittes Mal las. Gesagt getan, wenn auch etwas halbherzig.

Das Bilderbuch half mir, meine Sätze besser zu verbinden. Dies war ein wichtiger Meilenstein meines Lernprozesses Mir schien, als wäre Englisch ein Ozean mit unvorstellbaren Tiefen.

Da ich jedoch unbedingt die englische Sprache beherrschen wollte, konnte ich mit meinen Sprachkompetenzen nicht zufrieden sein.

Je mehr ich lernte, desto mehr Zeit wollte ich mit Sandy verbringen. Immer wenn wir uns sahen, fragte ich sie nach einer neuen Buchempfehlung. Sandy war eine sehr engagierte Lehrerin, und so hatte sie jedes Mal einen Tipp für mich. Mein Ziel war es, irgendwann ihr Sprachniveau zu erreichen.

Die Liebe zu Büchern, welche ich mittlerweile entwickelt hatte, schuf eine Verbindung zwischen uns. Am Wochenende trafen wir uns immer an einem bestimmten Platz im Park, an dem wir unsere Bücher lasen.

Mit der Zeit kamen wir uns näher und es kam zu einigen leichten Küssen. Neben den Büchern bauten wir etwas Intimität auf, was zu unserem ersten Date führte.

Es war Wochen her, seitdem sie mich mit den Kinder-Kurzgeschichten konfrontiert hatte, und jetzt wurde ich auf Science-Fiction-Bücher hochgestuft.

Das erste Date führte zum zweiten Date und das zweite zum dritten. Lustige, zurückhaltende Romantik und freier Ausdruck waren das, was unsere Dates schmückte.

Offiziell waren wir nun ein Paar. Sie gehörte mir und ich gehörte ihr. Was als Buchherausforderung begann, verwandelte sich in eine Liebesaffäre. Für mich war das eine unvorstellbar tolle Situation, in der ich mich befand. Nun waren Worte nicht mehr nur Worte, sie hatten eine tiefere und bildliche Bedeutung.

Sie war die Prinzessin und ich der Ritter in glänzender Rüstung, der kam um sie zu retten.

In unserer Beziehung war Englisch der Verbindungsknoten, unser Mittelpunkt, wo all unsere Gefühle ihren Ursprung hatten.

Es war unsere Brücke, unsere Grundlinie. In der Schule spiegelte sich dies wieder, ich war bald der beste Schüler der Klasse.

Selbst mathematische Wissenschaften hatten einen Aspekt der Sprache in sich und sie konnte nicht erfolgreich absolviert werden, wenn man die englische Sprache nicht beherrschte.

Wenn ich gebeten wurde mathematische Theorien zu erklären oder zu präsentieren, befähigte mich die Sprache, sie in der einfachsten und genauesten Form zu erklären.

Eineinhalb Jahre später hatte Englisch mir so viele Möglichkeiten in meinem neuen Leben eröffnet. Ein wichtiger Teil in diesem Wachstumsprozess war Sandy, die auch eine verborgene Leidenschaft für Sprache hatte.

Sie schlug vor, dass wir unsere Sprachstandards auf den Punkt des Intellektualismus und der künstlerischen Fähigkeiten hochschrauben. Wir beschlossen, Theaterstücke, Theateraufführungen und Gedichtnarrationen zu besuchen.

Ein paar Straßenblöcke weiter vom Restaurant entfernt befand sich ein Gemeinschaftstheater, das allen offenstand, die das Bedürfnis verspürten, die darstellenden Künste zu erkunden.

Die meisten Einheimischen lehnten das Theater als eine Allee für Amateure ab, aber wir respektierten jede Ideologie, die ein Individuum über die Sprache hatte, weshalb es wichtig war, ihnen eine faire Chance zu geben, um sich zu beweisen.

Wir waren hauptsächlich da, um zuzuhören, nicht um aufzutreten. Ich fand die künstlerische Sprache, die auf

Skripten geschrieben war, sehr tiefgründig und emotional. Ich konnte nicht anders, als sie tiefer zu untersuchen.

Wir entwickelten auch ein großes Interesse für Fernsehsendungen, Serien und jede lyrisch tiefgründige Musik.

Samstagabende wurden zu Theaterabenden für Sandy und mich. Es war eine gute Möglichkeit auszugehen und gleichzeitig unsere Sprache zu bereichern. Das Theater war nur von wenigen Leuten besucht, da es sehr alt war.

Wir wurden also Stammgäste im Theater. Schon bald kannten die Regisseure unsere Namen. Durch weitere Interaktion konnten wir lernen, wie Drehbuchautoren jedes Wort, das sie schreiben, selbst empfinden. Jedes Wort ist ein Teil des ganzen Systems. Wir waren so engagiert, dass es sogar unser Reden zwischen uns und anderen Menschen beeinträchtigte.

Sonntagabende wurden zu unserer Filmnacht, in der wir die am besten bewerteten Drehbuchfilme auswählten und ein großes Interesse an der Rede der Figur bekundeten. Die Sprache hatte meine Denkweise erweitert; sie hatte auch meine Beziehungen zu anderen verbessert. Ich fand es einfacher, Freunde zu finden, indem ich mit ihnen lustige Gespräche führte, was mich sympathisch machte. Worte schienen die Herzen der Menschen zu öffnen und sich für sie zu erwärmen. Im Gegenzug begann ich, das Zusammensein zu genießen und brach aus meinem introvertierten Kokon aus.

Dies führte zu meiner Wahl zum Studentenführer. Es fühlte sich erfüllend an, dass ich meinen Kameraden in einer offiziellen Funktion dienen konnte. Das Reden in der Öffentlichkeit war mein neu entdecktes Hobby.

Meine Besessenheit vom Englischen schuf jedoch eine Diskrepanz mit meiner polnischen Kultur.

Je seltener ich polnisch sprach, desto weniger Bedeutung hatte mein kultureller Hintergrund für mich. Ich hatte Amerika immer bewundert, aber zu keinem Zeitpunkt wollte ich meine polnische Persönlichkeit verlieren.

Meine polnischen Studienkollegen hatten mich bereits davor gewarnt und es traf mich härter als gedacht. Mir wurde klar, dass ich eine Weile lang kein polnisch gesprochen hatte.

Ich wollte ab sofort beide Sprachen gleich behandeln. Um beide Sprachen fließend sprechen zu können habe ich Übersetzungskurse besucht, in denen ich gelernt habe Polnisch in Englisch zu übersetzen und umgekehrt.

Die Unterscheidungskraft der beiden Sprachen war klar. Mein Hauptziel dabei war es, eine Verbindung zwischen den beiden Sprachen zu finden. Ein ausgeglichenes Individuum zu sein, das beide Sprachen fließend sprechen kann. Es stellte einen Teil dessen dar, wer ich war und wer ich werden wollte. In meinem letzten Studienjahr hatte ich mich an die

USA gewöhnt, so sehr, dass das Verlassen zu schwierig geworden war. Mein Visum sollte bald ablaufen und ich wäre gezwungen nach Polen zurückzukehren. Nicht, dass ich etwas dagegen hätte in Polen zu sein, aber ich hatte das Gefühl, dass ich in den USA Zuhause bin.

Nach gründlichen Überlegungen entschied ich mich dazu, einen Podcast zu starten. Podcasts waren ein neuer Trend der Massenmedien, der im Volksmund als „Radio on demand"; bekannt war.

Das Ziel war es, jeden Polen der nach Amerika kommt zu erreichen und ihn zu einem tollen Leben zu verhelfen. Ich musste zuerst meine Visumsfrage klären und beantragte eine Arbeitserlaubnis, damit ich Arbeit finden und alleine leben konnte.

Die meisten Studenten in dem Stipendium hatten es schwer, ihren Aufenthalt in den Staaten zu verlängern. Das ganze Verfahren zur Verlängerung meines Visums und meiner Arbeitserlaubnis führte zu einer verrückten Idee, welche natürlich von Sandy abstammte. Sie machte den Vorschlag, dass wir heiraten könnten, um mich so einbürgern zu lassen. Ich war mir erst nicht sicher, aber ich habe Sandy doch geliebt. Wir hatten doch schon genug Zeit miteinander verbracht.

Ich musste eine schnelle Entscheidung treffen, da mein Visum fast abgelaufen war. Leider würde unsere Ehe nicht eine dieser ausgefallenen sein, sondern nur eine einfache Bürgerrechtsvereinigung bei der Staatsanwaltschaft.

Wir fuhren also in Begleitung meiner beiden Trauzeugen Syzmon und Podolski zum Zivilamt, während sie ihre beiden Schwestern mitbrachte, um unsere Vereinigung zu bezeugen.

Ich hatte mir das Ganze nicht so vorgestellt, denn die Hochzeit sollte doch besonders und perfekt sein.

Die Zeremonie war kurz, wir legten unsere Gelübde ab und unterschrieben die Heiratsurkunden. Automatisch wurde ich offiziell amerikanischer Staatsbürger. Vor allem sollte ich für den Rest meines Lebens bei Sandy bleiben. Ich zog also mit ihr zusammen. Jetzt konnte ich meine Podcast-Pläne verfolgen, ich war entschlossen, die Herzen junger polnischer Jugendlicher zu berühren und ihnen den Übergang in die USA zu erleichtern.

Meine erste Herausforderung war es, einen geeigneten Namen für meinen Podcast zu finden. Nach langen Überlegungen entschied ich mich für den Namen „The Polish Podcast, for poles by poles“.

Der Podcast war speziell für Polen gedacht, die zur Arbeit oder zum Studium in die USA ziehen wollten.

Ich beschloss, den Podcast mit Interviews verschiedener Polen aufzupeppen, die in die USA gezogen sind und bereits alles durchlebt hatten. Ich habe auch etwas polnische Kultur und Stolz wie den polnischen Jazz und einige polnische Köstlichkeiten beigefügt. Ich habe Polen in den USA vermarktet und gleichzeitig die Gastfreundschaft der Staaten gegenüber Ausländern gelobt. Es war nicht einfach, eine Fanbase aufzubauen, die meisten Zuhörer waren Polen aus meinem College. Der Podcast ist der Ort, an dem ich all meine erstaunlichen Erfahrungen meines Aufenthalts in Amerika teilte.

Es war erstaunlich, welche Dinge ich mit meinen Ambitionen für die englische Sprache erreicht hatte.

Sandy und ich haben gut trainiert und aufgrund meiner hervorragenden Noten wurde mir eine vertragliche Tutorenstelle an der Hochschule angeboten, um allen Schülern zu helfen, die Schwierigkeiten im Unterricht hatten.

Mein Abschluss war eine bunte Zeremonie mit meinen Eltern, die aus Polen kamen um an meinem Erfolg teilzuhaben.

Wenn ich an die Vergangenheit denke, habe ich meinen ganzen Erfolg einem kleinen Feuer in mir zu verdanken, welches funkelte als ich die englische Sprache entdeckte.

# Haftungsausschluss

Die Umsetzung aller enthaltenen Informationen, Anleitungen und Strategien dieses E-Books erfolgt auf eigenes Risiko. Für etwaige Schäden jeglicher Art kann der Autor aus keinem Rechtsgrund eine Haftung übernehmen. Für Schäden materieller oder ideeller Art, die durch die Nutzung oder Nichtnutzung der Informationen bzw. durch die Nutzung fehlerhafter und/oder unvollständiger Informationen verursacht wurden, sind Haftungsansprüche gegen den Autor grundsätzlich ausgeschlossen. Ausgeschlossen sind daher auch jegliche Rechts- und Schadensersatzansprüche. Dieses Werk wurde mit größter Sorgfalt nach bestem Wissen und Gewissen erarbeitet und niedergeschrieben. Für die Aktualität, Vollständigkeit und Qualität der Informationen übernimmt der Autor jedoch keinerlei Gewähr. Auch können Druckfehler und Falschinformationen nicht vollständig ausgeschlossen werden. Für fehlerhafte Angaben vom Autor kann keine juristische Verantwortung sowie Haftung in irgendeiner Form übernommen werden.

# Urheberrecht

# Impressum



1. Auflage



Kontakt: Daniel Bell, Dünnebank 12, 59379 Selm

Layout und Satz: Adam Winterspoon

Printed in Germany
by Amazon Distribution
GmbH, Leipzig

16110534R00039